JE - B

D0436644

I am an Aro Publishing
Twenty Word Book

My twenty words are:

Holey	to
Moley	see
digs	the
a	pen
hole	barn
she	is
mole	corn
so	more
does	kitchen
fun	floor

ISBN 0-89868-159-6 — Library Bound
ISBN 0-89868-160-X — Soft Bound

FUNNY FARM BOOKS

Holey Moley Cow

Story by Wendy Kanno
Pictures by Bob Reese

ARO PUBLISHING

B

Holey Moley

digs a hole.

Holey Moley,

she is a mole!

Moles dig holes,

so does she.

Holey Moley is

fun to see.

Holey Moley

digs the pen.

Holey Moley

digs the barn.

Holey Moley

digs the pen.

Holey Moley

digs the corn.

Holey Moley!

She digs more.

Holey Moley digs

the kitchen floor!

0/11   5/0,   2-6-04